# White is the Moon

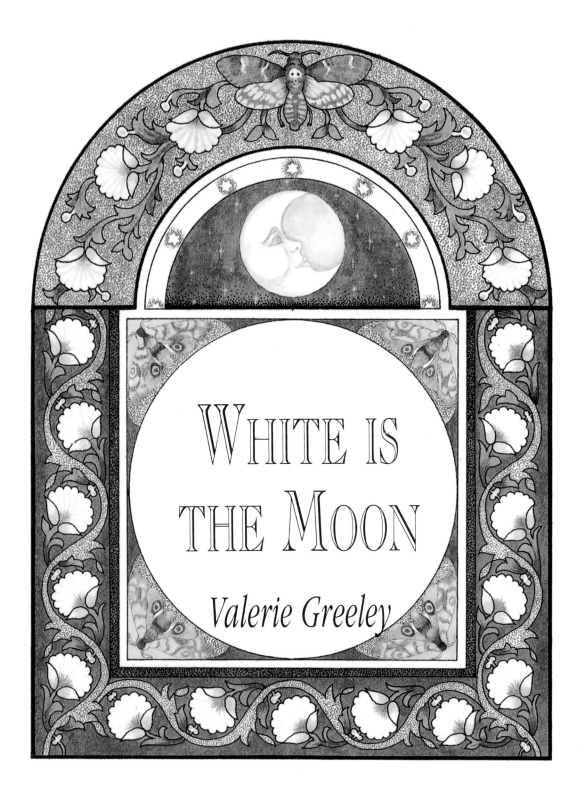

# WHITE IS THE MOON

*Valerie Greeley*

PictureLions

*An Imprint of* HarperCollins*Publishers*

White is the moon
Shining bright
Sees an owl
In the night

Brown is the owl
With steely stare
Sees a fox
Standing there

Red is the fox
Sly and fast
Sees a frog
Hopping past

Green is the frog
With glinting eyes
Sees the sun
Slowly rise

Yellow's the sun
Golden, bright
Sees a bird
Taking flight

Black is the bird
Swooping low
Sees a crab
Down below

Pink is the crab
Crawling up
Sees a seal
With her pup

Grey is the seal
Shining wet
Sees the sun
About to set

Orange the sun
Changing hue
Sees the sky
Changing too

Blue is the sky
In fading light
Sees the moon
Now say Goodnight!

First published in Great Britain by
Blackie and Son Limited in 1990
First published in Picture Lions in 1992
This edition published in 1992
Picture Lions is an imprint of the Children's Division,
part of HarperCollins Publishers Limited,
77-85 Fulham Palace Road, Hammersmith,
London W6 8JB

Printed in Great Britain